All This

Matters

By
Kayleigh Hughes

To all those, who haven't yet had to explain their search history.

CONTENTS

ONE

Marie strode towards the podium on the assembly hall stage. She straightened the collar on her slim-fit purple blazer, as her curly grey hair bounced on her shoulders, gazing over the many rows of new students before her. Bright and eager, like they should have been. Well, most of them. Some fidgeted. Coughed. Couldn't sit still, as was to be expected. Yawned. Some other teachers stood on either side along the walls, monitoring the students. Ready to step in, in case things went balls-up.

By the fifth year in Marie's twenty year career, this speech was as familiar to her as her and Dana's drive to and from work. Of course, Dana wasn't here. She was likely immersed with mending yet another piece of equipment up in her office. Apparently, Sandford College's entire computer system was due to be updated next week. If the countless memos sent out to everyone in the last week were anything to go by.

Because, no matter what, someone always missed the message.

Marie cleared her throat.

'Good morning, everyone.'

'Good morning,' the students chorused.

'I'd like to welcome you all to Sandford College,' Marie began. 'Most of you will have already met me, Mrs Gordon, your Head of Year and the Head of Pastoral Care. I, along with the rest of the staff, will strive to ensure your time here is valued, and for every student to achieve their best. That no student will be left out. To assure you that, every year until you leave, I'll be here, Mr Niblock the safeguarding leader, and your form teachers, will be here. Whenever you may need help, or maybe just want someone to talk to. In everything we do, it is you the students who are put first.'

The words rolled off Marie's tongue, but never sounded rehearsed. That, she was positively sure of. As was the principal, Nathan Byrne. A well-built man who stood as tall as he did proud, at the side of the stage, his silver hair slicked back as always. Proud of how the school thrived; its unwavering popularity. As it should have been.

'I'll pass things over to Mr Byrne now. Thank you.'

Marie stepped aside, flashing a smile, then down off the stage as the man approached the podium. Eleanor Conway gave Marie a quick nod as she joined the other teachers.

Watching Nathan do his bit like it was nothing.

* * *

Marie walked towards the assembly hall doors alongside numerous groups of students. She exited, heading down the corridor towards the main office. Sharon sat behind the desk, scribbling something down on a notebook.

'All right, Sharon? Listen, got a few things I need sent-'

'Mrs Gordon?'

Marie turned. A small boy stood before her, clutching a sheet of paper.

'Just a minute, Sharon. You all right, Owen?'

The boy shuffled his feet, seemingly doing his best not to look at the floor.

'I'm, uh, I'm just a bit worried about something, Miss.'

'What is it?'

Owen met her eyes - Marie's warm tone seemed to have put him at ease.

'I haven't, uh, got any of my friends here. I don't wanna walk to classes on my own.'

Marie nodded.

'Have you not got talking to any of the other students yet?'

Owen shook his head. 'Not really.'

Marie paused, looking at the boy as his gaze returned to the floor.

'Okay. Well, why don't you try doing that during your first few classes? Or even in your form class or at break or lunch?'

Owen initially glanced at her, then looked up.

'Okay.'

Marie nodded, smiling at him. 'Just see how that goes. But if you've no luck, just come to me, and I can see about maybe having someone walk with you, even just to your classes, all right?'

Owen smiled a bright smile.

'Okay, Miss.'

Marie exchanged the smile, stepping back.

'What's your next class?'

'English, Miss.'

And for period six before lunch, Marie's History class.

'Know where you're going?'

Owen looked at the piece of paper.

'D4, Miss, but I can't-'

Marie turned, spotting a younger woman in the foyer.

'Ruth?'

The woman walked towards them.

'Would you take Owen here to D4 for his class?'

'Sure, no problem.'

Ruth led Owen away. Marie turned back to the main office.

'Always one, isn't there?' Sharon quipped.

Marie chuckled quietly.

'Ah, it happens. Anyway, got some things I need sent down from resources...'

* * *

Dana sat upright at her desk. Sheets, leads, and cables, amidst other things swamped her workspace. She unplugged a lead from Mary Harris' projector. Another one done. Over these last two months, she almost wished that Harris was the one with the degree in computers. Almost. Dana untied her red hair, ruffled it a little, then retied it. She lifted the projector and headed out of her office and down what was definitively the longest corridor in the school. Several students passed by, followed by Leanne Preston, the head of Home Economics. Almost as bad as Harris in the technology department.

'All right, Dana?'

'Aye.'

Dana continued on, reaching the first door at the end of the corridor. Open as usual, since it could never actually be shut properly. Dana appeared to have caught Harris during a free period, given no students were present. She stood at her full lanky height, knocking gently.

'All right, Mary?'

Harris looked up from her paperwork, as Dana set the projector down.

'All sorted. That should be it all working now.'

'Ah, great stuff. Thanks, Dana.'

'Just remember not to leave it on over night next time, all right?'

Harris nodded.

'Any other issues,' Dana continued. 'I'll be here to about half four. Just give us a bell, all right?'

'No problem. Thanks again, Dana.'

She nodded then left, turning back up the way she came, this time stopping at the last door on the right. It was also open, though not quite enough to know if occupied or not. Dana pushed it slightly, peeping her head round.

'Hiya, Dana.'

Ah, Cathryn Redmond. Just the one Dana was looking for. Cathryn stood at a filing cabinet behind her desk. Her black crop was neat as ever, unlike her navy blouse which they both knew was beginning to have seen better days. In fact, her attire had been a little more casual lately – almost as much as Dana's green and black checkered shirt and denim jeans.

'Got something for me?'

'Yep,' Cathryn said brightly, handing over her laptop.

'Tell you something, Cathryn, that was a wild one back on Saturday, wasn't it?'

Cathryn chuckled.

'Oh, I know,' she said. 'Siobhan could hardly balance herself after her second vodka.'

'She could hardly get out of bed the whole next day, for her head was thumping. I had to come over and play nurse.'

The two women exchanged a giggle.

'Ah sure,' Cathryn said, 'not long until the Christmas one, eh? Ade won't know what to do with himself in that house.'

Dana chuckled, tucking the laptop under her arm.

'I'll get on to this as soon as I can. Shouldn't be too long.'

Cathryn flashed her a smile.

'I mean, it should hold out until your new one comes, so I don't think you'll have to worry too much.'

'Will that still be in December, or...?'

'Nah, probably sometime in the new year at this point. Bit of a backlog.'

Cathryn nodded, then turned back to the cabinet.

'See you tomorrow, Cathryn .'

'See you.'

* * *

'All right, everyone. Settle down. Settle down.'

Cathryn walked across her classroom to her desk, clutching a blue folder under her arm, not even glancing at the eighteen students before her. 10R. Her favourite class - not. At least a third of the class hated History, so it was already a given that they'd be glad never to have set foot in Cathryn's room after this year.

Gradually, the noise died down as she took her seat and started up her laptop. A little on the slow side for the last while, but hopefully Dana would know what was up with it. Fingers crossed it was nothing *too* problematic. Cathryn reached for a small remote and pointed it up at the projector.

'Has everyone got their booklets with them? We're onto slavery today.'

The rustling of eighteen booklets, though more like eighteen-hundred, being taken out of school bags and set upon each desk rippled through the classroom.

'Are we watching a video today, Miss?'

'Nope. We have to get through these booklets first. If everyone could copy down from the powerpoint, please.'

'When are we doing racism?' another student asked, as most began writing. 'You know, the people in the white pointy cloaks?'

Cathryn could almost feel her eyes rolling. It was going to be a long year.

'That's the Ku Klux Klan,' she replied flatly.

'We'll be doing all that after Halloween.'

Numerous enthused murmurs sounded around the room. Cathryn scoffed into herself. Maybe some would have a change of heart after all.

'It wasn't them who killed Martin Luther King, was it?' a third student asked.

'Could you just start writing please, Martin?'

The boy did as such. Cathryn glanced up at the clock. Five past ten.

'How far along is everyone?'

'Third line.'

'Second sentence.'

'End of the first paragraph.'

Cathryn nodded as the class continued writing. She could already taste the extra-strong coffee she'd be filling her mug with in twenty-five minutes. The sooner she could have a cigarette as well, the better.

TWO

'No joke, they were up again to about four o'clock arguing. Sometimes I wish I spoke Slovakian.'

Dana practically guffawed as Marie shook her head. The latter evidently couldn't help but share Dana's amusement, still managing to focus on the road ahead.

'That is mental,' Dana quipped. 'How long'd you say it's been happening, again? About four months?'

'Aye, thereabouts. You'd think they'd maybe wait until the day time when everyone's out.'

'Bloody hell, you've got paper-thin walls, as well. Can you not tell them to pack it in?'

'They'd have to teach me some of their lovely language first.'

Dana chuckled.

'You'll be glad to get away from it for a bit at the weekend, I'm sure.'

Marie exhaled with relief.

'Oh, I'm already there.'

'The Maldives,' Dana said brightly. 'Better than anywhere Siobhan and I have been.'

'She's always been more of a home bird, hasn't she?'

Dana nodded. 'Aye. But you know, works for us.'

'Neither Eric or I have forgotten, at least. You remember Sarah Letson's fella did on their fifteenth. Nearly got the face ate off him.'

Dana scoffed lightly.

'Best way to never forget: have it the same week as your birthday.'

'Aye, yeah, that's right. It was your thirty-fifth, was it?'

'Yep,' Dana chuckled. 'Have to make sure never to buy Siobhan flowers, though.'

'Why, does she go off on a big strop or something?'

Dana shook her head.

'Allergic.'

Marie smiled. 'Ah, yeah.'

'Except now it's dandelions and daffodils too. Your Eric's a very lucky man. Been nineteen years now, hasn't it?'

'Twenty. And both only being twenty-six when we met – just babies.'

'And I thought we were doing good at twelve years together.'

'Oh you are, for only seeing the arse of each other every few weeks. Don't know if I could manage that long.'

The car slowed down as it came to a red light. Dana glanced at Marie as she drummed her fingers on the wheel. The urge to learn herself had always just completely passed Dana by. Nerves or maybe road rage would possibly have gotten the better of her, anyway. Fortunately Marie was quite the accomplished driver, having helped even her husband pass with flying colours. Cathryn could be a bit of maniac - you didn't dare try to be a backseat driver with her. Both did seem to keep their cars clean enough, though - the bubblegum air freshener in Marie's was a bonus.

The light turned green and onwards they went.

'Tell you what. I'm looking forward to Eric's linguini when I get back.'

'The one you said tastes like rubber?'

Marie nudged Dana, who shot her a playful smile.

'Making the most before before you have to endure all that foreign shit, eh?'

'It's not bad actually,' Marie countered. 'How often do you get to have a cocktail so early in the morning over here?'

Dana chuckled, a little louder than intended.

'I hope you spoil him, I really do.'

Marie glanced at her in the corner of her eye.

'Oh, you *bet* I will.'

* * *

Dana climbed out of Marie's car, waving her off, and headed up the pathway to her front door. After the week she'd had in work, Siobhan's company would be more than welcome. She had spoken rather enthusiastically about the new camera she had obtained just last week, so no doubt there would be some interesting snaps on display tonight. Dana shut the door behind her and headed up the stairs, turning right into a small bedroom. She approached a brown wardrobe and removed a t-shirt and bottoms, then shifted the remaining clothes in the wardrobe to one side. As always, there was enough room for Siobhan's.

Now changed, Dana returned downstairs and went into the kitchen. She took out two plates from a cupboard, then-

Heard the lock click. The door opened. Dana smiled.

'What time do you call this?'

Siobhan shared Dana's smile, striding towards her. Her blonde bob fortunately hadn't changed, nor her brown leather jacket and black jeans which she always pulled off so well. Siobhan blew a raspberry before exchanging a kiss on the lips.

'Wait until you hear about my week,' she remarked.

'Wait until you hear about mine.'

Siobhan chuckled, glancing at the plates.

'So, Heston Blumenthal, what's on the menu?'

'I was thinking...chow mein. Just from the usual.'

Siobhan let out a little smile.

'Oh. Sounds good,' she said, then headed out along the hallway. 'I'll just go and get my stuff.'

Two whole nights with this ever delightful woman. Dana was going to savour every moment as it would be a good while until the next time. That's what always worked best.

Dana listened as footsteps thudded down the stairs.

'Left the camera in the car! If I had brains...'

Dana chuckled as Siobhan's voice trailed away. Between that and breaking wind just a little bit more often than Dana would have liked, thank bloody Christ for single beds.

Dana opened a drawer, took out a menu, then headed towards the landline in the hall.

* * *

15

Marie pulled into the driveway outside her house. A big brown semi-detached house on Eden Road. Hopefully the Slovakian folk next door were out. Marie climbed out and walked to the white front door. It could have done with a fresh coat, but at present there were more important things.

Marie pushed open the door. Eric came down the last step, combing back his long, slightly-greying, dark hair. A good bit over six foot, but not quite as handsome as in his younger days. You just had to take the rough with the smooth.

'All right, love?' Eric said.

Marie smiled, closing the door gently. Just in case the Slovakians were in fact at home.

'Any more from that lot?'

Eric shook his head.

'Nah. Looks like we might get a bit of peace before Saturday.'

Marie's face lit up.

'So we can get a bit of action up there tonight, then?'

Eric sighed, smiling.

'Twenty years, Marie. Let's make it a good one.'

She flashed him a smile then headed up the stairs, as Eric continued down the hallway into the kitchen. Marie quickly changed from her work attire to a far more comfortable black vest top and blue leggings, lifted her phone, then returned down stairs and into the living room. She sat down on their one and only sofa, glancing at her phone. Given he wasn't much of a phone user, Eric had predictably left his upstairs. He saw them mostly as a distraction – which was just as well with him being head cook in this house.

'I hope you'll have enough of that perfume left until Sunday, love. That's your best one.'

'How about I douse our pillows with it tonight?'

Eric chuckled.

Dinner'll be ready in about twenty minutes. Going to have omelettes instead.'

Even better than linguini.

'Righto.'

He returned into the kitchen.

Marie lounged back. That would give her a little extra energy to mark 9H's books. And even more for up in the bedroom later on.

* * *

Cathryn walked in through the front door. She dropped her bag to the side.

'In here, Cath!'

As always. Cathryn removed her coat, hung it on the bannister, then headed into the living room. Adrian sat diagonally on the sofa, appearing to read the paper. Or possibly yesterday's paper, just to bide the time until *Coronation Street*. She plopped herself down on the other end, glancing at the balding man.

'How was work today, then?'

Cathryn sighed.

'Oh, I'll just be glad to have a fag soon.'

She rubbed her eyes as Adrian folded the paper.

'Want your coffee, aye?'

Cathryn nodded. Adrian stood up and exited out into the kitchen. Cathryn reached for the remote. Four minutes to eight. Good timing. She raised her hand to her head and lifted off her crop, rubbing her smooth head. Breathed a sigh of relief. Once she made the move to a head scarf, things would be even better.

Cathryn inhaled as the rich cappuccino aroma drifted into the room.

'Where's Jake, then, Ade?' she asked as Adrian passed her the mug. 'Still working?'

'Aye. Just started a couple of hours ago.'

Adrian sat on the other end, turning to the screen, just as the *Coronation Street* played. Cathryn blew on her mug.

'He's been fairly quiet lately.'

'Well, since you're never both in the house together, Cath...'

'Aye, but he'd had a day off yesterday. He could have talked to me then.'

Adrian shrugged, gaze fixed on the television. Cathryn sighed loudly, before taking a couple of sips.

'He's going to be twenty-two in a few months, for Christ's sake.

'He's been staying with Jessica.'

'Oh, right.'

'Think she wants a kid at some point.'

Cathryn snorted. Adrian glanced at her.

'You didn't know what you wanted until-'

She shot him a 'touché' look.

'When will he be in?'

'Think about five.'

Cathryn sipped again. 'Does she really?'

Despite that her voice had softened, Adrian didn't look away from the screen.

'That's what I've heard.'

Cathryn sighed. 'Right.'

Was that why, though? Or was it what both she and Adrian strongly sensed it to be? Cathryn placed her mug to the side, then arose.

'Going for my fag.'

Adrian nodded as Cathryn left. Oh, she couldn't wait.

THREE

'Somehow she ripped the door off its hinges. By accident, too, apparently.'

Cathryn rolled her eyes and sighed at what was just one of Amanda McGreevy's recollections of a pretty hectic October morning. They sat, along with Graham Niblock and Sandra Pellingham, amidst the lunchtime buzz in the staffroom. Amanda took a forkful of her plate of pasta bake from the canteen. Sandra sipped on her bottle of orange juice, chuckling into herself. Graham rubbed his eyes, setting his salad container aside, just as Cathryn reached into her bag hanging over her chair, removing a pack of cigarettes and lighter.

'How in the name of god did she manage that?' Cathryn asked.

Amanda exhaled.

'Honestly do not know, Cath. Hinges must've been pretty bloody loose.'

'Was it definitely an accident?' Graham asked.

Amanda ate another bite.

'Somehow. *Somehow.*'

Graham lifted bottle from the side of his chair.

'I'm surprised that hasn't happened to our back door, with the number of times the kid next door has kicked his ball against it. They're going away for the weekend, at least, though.'

'Got anything planned yourself, Graham?' Amanda asked.

'Nah, not this one. But next weekend it's our Charlotte's wedding. Can't wait.'

'You'll have a well good time,' said Sandra. 'Just hope you won't still be legless come the Monday.'

Cathryn and Amanda snorted. Sandra took another sip of orange juice.

'Suppose it'll be a quiet one for you, then, Cath?'

Cathryn nodded, tapping her pack of cigarettes with her finger.

'Aye, but Ade knows what he'll be at. I'm just glad Jake's not done any more four hour bike rides at half-one in the morning, since he's been working.'

Amanda chuckled.

'I still cannot believe he did that. I'd be tucked well away in my bed.'

'Must be a male thing, eh, Graham?' Sandra quipped.

Graham scoffed. 'Aye, right.'

Amanda munched on another forkful of her pasta bake, just as Marie walked past.

'Here, Marie, are you and Eric still heading away on Saturday for your anniversary?'

Marie turned, her face brightening.

'Oh, yes,' she replied brightly. 'Going all in at the Maldives. He really knows how to spoil me, so he does.'

'Nice one,' Graham said.

'Can't wait to see the photos,' Sandra chuckled.

Marie grinned, then continued on. Cathryn placed her packet of cigarettes in her pocket, and stood up.

'Be back shortly.'

The other three nodded and she headed towards the back door.

* * *

Marie walked towards reception.

'All right, Sharon? Any word about Lewis O'Neill's dad getting back to us yet?'

Sharon stopped typing, looking at her notebook.

'No, nothing yet. Lewis said his dad's working to about five, but he might find a moment to call us before then.'

'Right, okay. Thanks, Sharon.'

Sharon flashed Marie a smile, who then turned and headed to the staffroom, just as Cathryn Redmond was heading in the same direction.

'Ah, Cathryn. Everything still on course for the presentation tomorrow?'

'Yep. There's a few who'll need a bit of extra time. Just the usual ones.'

Marie nodded.

'Right. Good, good.'

'I'll keep you posted if...'

'Sure.'

They exchanged a nod, then Cathryn moved on towards the principal's office and Marie went into the staffroom.

* * *

'They're giving me about seven months, tops. The doctor said it's pretty far along.'

Cathryn cleared her throat, as she sat opposite Nathan in his office. The urge to remove her wig prodded relentlessly at her, but for professionalism's sake, she stuck it out.

Nathan nodded, drumming his fingers on the desk.

'We don't have to make a big show of this, regardless of how many may already know,' he said. 'But I imagine your colleagues will want to do something, even if it's just a card and flowers.'

Cathryn sighed, then nodded. It was always the way. She didn't want to go off so soon. Didn't want to be at home. Even though Cathryn and Adrian had agreed for her final days to be in hospital, a part of her didn't want it be the last thing she saw. Even though it wouldn't. She'd have Adrian, at least, because god knows where Jake was at.

'They said, time and time again, that I should've stopped the fags. But of course, did I listen? How soon would you suggest that I leave?'

Nathan leaned back, exhaling.

'I mean, it's up to you, Cathryn, but given what stage your cancer's at, maybe it should be sooner.'

'Right.'

Nathan leaned forward, looking Cathryn straight in the eyes.

'I know - I *know* - this is difficult for you, and it will be for everyone else as well. I think some of the students especially will miss you more than they'd let on.'

Cathryn half-smiled.

'I'm sure.'

Nathan placed his hand on the desk.

'I know you'd been dreading having to have this conversation,' he said softly. 'And I don't want to sound like I'm waving you off already, Cathryn, but...just think of the difference you've made for so many of our students over the last twenty-nine years. Everything you've done. Just remember that.'

Nathan was right. It had been incredibly rewarding and she had met and known some people. But Cathryn couldn't think about that. Instead lingered the thought of the hospital walls. Because she hadn't cut back enough. Adrian hadn't wanted to nag too much, but maybe he should have. Maybe Jake should have, as well.

Cathryn nodded.

'Thanks, Nathan.'

* * *

Marie climbed into her car and shut the door. One of the more hectic January afternoons. You never could have every student just sit still and behave themselves, of course. Evidently if the presentation had been on something most of them actually wanted to give even an iota of their interest in. Different strokes...

Marie spied her watch. Half past four. Plenty of time. She took out her phone.

'Hi, Eric. Listen, I'm going to be late again. Bit of a more crazy day than usual.'

'I'll leave something out for you, and you can just heat it up, all right?'

'Sure.'

'When do you reckon, love, about half-six?'

'Aye, probably, if nothing else holds me up.'

'All right, see you later, love.'

'See you then.'

Marie dumped the phone aside, then started the car and drove away.

Fifteen minutes later, the car pulled up outside the last of a row of bungalows in Dane Street. Just five minutes from Eden Road. Marie caught herself in the rear view mirror. She pushed either side of her grey curls back. Straightened the collar of her blouse. Flashed herself a smile. Marie opened the door and climbed out, heading towards the short path leading to the front door. She strode up towards the door, removing a key from her pocket, then turned it in the keyhole quietly, though not that that mattered. Marie entered, closing the door behind her.

'Hello, darling.'

Her tone was playful - eager - as always.

Harvey sat upright on the bottom of the staircase. Slim and sumptuously blonde, and just a little taller – and a good ten years younger – than Marie. He shared her smile of delight as he climbed to his feet, holding out his ever soft hand.

He led the way up the stairs, turning left across the landing. Marie giggled as they reached a blue door at the end. Harvey reached for the handle and gradually opened the door. He gently pulled Marie inside and she followed, letting out more giggles as she shut it behind them.

* * *

Dana sat across the sofa, with her arm around Siobhan as the latter rested against her. Dana lifted her glass of ginger beer from beside the sofa, taking a couple of sips. Their first of three nights together this week.

'Wonder how many of us would actually be like Frank Grimes,' Dana said, 'if Homer was in the real world?'

Siobhan chuckled, just as Frank Grimes was about to grab the high voltage cables.

'...don't need safety gloves because I'm...'

'I think I would. He's a bigger idiot than that Spanish fella down the road.'

Dana snorted.

'Aye, but he wouldn't get into space like Homer,' she replied. 'Though, at least he's not as annoying as Bart. That kid can be a real prat sometimes.'

'Bit like some of the ones in Sandford, it sounds like.'

'Aye, so some of the teachers say. Utter madhouse.'

The two women laughed just as Frank Grimes' coffin was lowered into the ground, like those present at his funeral.

'Bet you're glad you don't have to deal with them.'

Dana scoffed, taking a sip of her ginger beer.

'The teachers can be bloody worse,' she said. 'That McGreevy woman spends more time in my office than where she's supposed to be.'

'Maybe they should get someone like that teacher who replaces Lisa's one – the substitute.'

'You mean the one voiced by Dustin Hoffman?'

'Aye. Mr Bergstrom I think you called him.'

Dana nodded.

'Could've done with more like him in my school days. Wouldn't have had any dusters being fired at you.'

Siobhan snorted then let out a giggle.

'Wonder would that shut Bart up?'

'Bet not,' Dana quipped. 'Wouldn't have gotten twenty-odd seasons out of it, otherwise. It'll be the year 5000 before it stops.'

'I wonder what the beer tastes like? Better than that shite your necking down your gob, I bet.'

Dana elbowed Siobhan then took a big sip. Maybe it tasted like piss. Maybe it was the best thing ever. Siobhan arose, stretching her legs.

'Going to the little girls room. Don't start the next one 'til I get back.'

Dana gave her a thumbs up, then took another sip.

FOUR

Dana stood at the sink in her office, rinsing a mug. Despite this unusually milder February, she couldn't go without her hot tea. Most staff had gone home now, and so would she, soon enough. Sinead McKillop's speakers still hadn't been looked at, and she would need them by Friday. It wouldn't actually take too long, but Dana had endured a rather hectic day, so it would just have to wait until tomorrow.

'I've done something.'

Dana turned, setting down the mug. Marie stood in the doorway, rubbing the back of her neck.

'What?'

'I didn't mean to, it was an accident.'

'What was?'

Marie paused. Inhaled. Dana keep her gaze on the other woman.

'What did you do, Marie?'

'I don't want him snitching – I don't-'

'What'd you do?'

Dana's tone was a little firmer than she had intended, it seemed.

'Marie, what did you do?'

She met Dana's gaze, lowering her shoulders.

'Pushed him. I-got-angry-at-him-and-pushed him.'

'Who?'

'George Doyle. He's a lad in Year Nine.'

'What, you think he'll report you?'

'I didn't mean – I overreacted and I... I don't know.'

Dana put out her hand, in some attempt to calm the other woman down.

'When'd it happen?'

'Yesterday. I don't want him sni-'

'What is it you want me to do, Marie? Why have you told me?'

Marie exhaled.

'I don't want that boy snitching.'

'Marie, what is it you want me to do?'

Marie shook her head. Dana straightened herself up.

'Wait, did you say it happened yesterday?'

'Yeah.'

'Well, has Nathan spoken to you, or, I don't know, have there been any calls to the school or....?'

Marie shook her head.

'The kid mustn't have said anything, then. I mean, you know how fast things travel around this place.'

Pause.

'Why'd you tell me, then?'

Marie exhaled and shook her head, waving her hand. Dana stuck her hand in her trouser pocket.

'If it was just an accident – a one-off – and Nathan's not onto you, things'll probably be all right.'

Marie nodded.

'Yeah.'

Dana removed her hand from her pocket and turned back to her desk.

Marie exited the office.

* * *

Cathryn held her phone to her ear, after an unsuccessful third call to her son.

'...leave a message after the tone.'

Beep.

Jake,' Cathryn began. 'It's your mother. I don't know what's been going on with you. Maybe if you could return this call, or better still, have a chat when you're here. Love you.'

Beep.

Cathryn hung up, sighing. She began to wonder if there was any point now. Maybe. Maybe he was just building up the moment, carefully deciding what he'd like to say. No. It probably hadn't even crossed his mind, knowing him.

So his girlfriend wanted a child? Did he? Did Jake understand – know – what kind of responsibility that would be? Cathryn herself hadn't known until her late twenties, and even then it was another few years when she, along with Adrian, finally decided the time was right. Now he was just spending all of his time with a woman he'd known for mere months. Couldn't bear to look at the one who had brought him into the world. At least only since he had known Jessica. Cathryn had nothing against her – not a thing – but sometimes she wondered. Had Jessica been saying things, putting ideas in Jake's head? Cathryn sincerely hoped not.

* * *

'Has he got next week off, then?'

Cathryn sat up in bed as Adrian climbed in next to her. He yawned a little, rubbing his arms. It had only been around an hour since her last cigarette, but now she needed another. Chemo seemed to be coming along all right, so why not?

'Yeah. Just to Monday.'

Cathryn folded her arms.

'He could do it before then.'

'Do what?'

'You *know* what,' she snapped. 'Honestly, what's he playing at?'

Adrian shrugged. 'Probably just tired, Cath.'

She snorted.

'I work a good few more hours than him, and you don't hear me complaining how knackered I am when I come home everyday.'

Adrian sniffed, letting out another yawn.

'I'll talk to him when he's back tomorrow.'

'*I* want to talk to him,' Cathryn sniped. 'I want to know what the hell is going on with our son.'

Adrian turned onto his side, half-looking at her.

'You don't need to get so worked up, Cath. He'll come round to you eventually.'

Cathryn stared at her husband. Oh, of course Jake would.

'Yeah? Yeah? What if he doesn't and then I'm gone?'

'Cath, will you stop worrying? It'll not do either of you any favours.'

Cathryn pulled off the duvet and climbed off the bed, stomping towards the door. Adrian looked to her.

'What are you-'

'Heading out for a fag, or two.'

Adrian grunted, turning back on his side as the door shut.

What was Jake playing at?

* * *

Dana stood at her desk, pressing some buttons on a laptop. She took a sip of tea. Almost a week had passed since that...odd revelation from Marie. With all the shit that went on in this place, though, it was probably just a blip on the radar by now. The door creaked.

'I did it again.'

Dana turned. Marie's face was almost blank. There was no quiver, no hesitation, in her voice. Dana paused.

'Again?'

'Yeah.'

Marie looked briefly at the floor as Dana stepped forward.

'Jesus Christ. You didn't mean to do it, *again*, Marie?'

'It wasn't the same kid.'

'It wasn't an accident this time.'

'I'm not having them find-'

'Why did you tell me? The first time, why?'

Marie paused. Looked at Dana. Grabbed her and twisted her arms behind her back, pinning the woman face down against the desk. Dana froze, eyes darting.

'I don't want them finding out about this,' Marie said flatly. 'The same way you wouldn't want them to know about your...little problem.'

Dana's voice caught several times in her throat.

'What... What do you-'

Marie turned Dana onto her back. Moved her finger swiftly across her throat. Dana swallowed at the woman's hardened stare.

'Jesus. They're just... Marie, they're just kids.'

'I know.'

Marie stood back. Dana pushed herself off the desk and to her feet. Marie walked towards the door.

'Both...Both of them?'

Marie turned, then nodded.

'How?'

'What?'

'How do you want me to do it?'

Marie paused.

'Meet me in the car, soon as you're done here.'

Dana glanced between Marie and the floor, feeling a shiver run down her spine.

'R-Right.'

Marie walked off.

FIVE

Cathryn exited the toilet cubicle and headed over to the sinks. The school day was over, but not her work day. She'd need another cigarette after this booster class with these Year Eleven students. There were definitely worse ones to deal with, to be fair, but hopefully they, as had always been the case in the past, would find it of some benefit.

Cathryn scrubbed her hands under the running water, then pulled out a few paper towels and dried them. As she dumped them in the bin, Cathryn felt something in her throat. Put her hand to her mouth as she hacked out a cough. Then another. Then another, each becoming drier and harsher. Louder. Cathryn approached a sink, as more coughs came out. She bent over, as each-

As blood spluttered into the sink.

She paused, looking at the red spots for several moments.

Pushed herself upright. Cathryn rinsed the sink, re-washed her hands, and left. She'd have to cut down, again.

* * *

Cathryn pushed the trolley down the half-empty poultry aisle. She never wanted to eat much, and when she did, it was all the same. Chicken. Eggs. Carrots and peas. The odd time, Cathryn tried to consume some crackers, but could never keep them down. She picked up a six pack of chicken breasts, almost throwing it into the trolley. Maybe next time she would accept Adrian's offer to accompany her. Or Jake's, if ever he bothered to show his face. Cathryn continued on to the fruit aisle, but longed to stop. Go home again. Day by day, this hellish fatigue weighed down harder and harder on her.

Three months left, but probably not even.

Cathryn passed a woman then a male couple. Next time, Adrian could drop her here and collect her again. The drive to and from work she could still manage, though.

Cathryn lifted a packet of strawberries and a bunch of bananas. Before chemo, she couldn't stand either, but now loved them. Beetroot had once been a favourite, but now she absolutely *hated* it. Even more than the stench of Adrian's breath after a few. Cathryn coughed

- just the once, this time. She took out a list from her pocket. Sighed. She was going to be here a little longer than planned.

* * *

The front door swung open and Dana staggered through. She continued down the hallway, letting it shut, just as she came to the bathroom. Dana stumbled towards the toilet, lifted up the lid and heaved. Yellow and orange exploded from her mouth into the bowl. Again. Again. The pungent stench almost threatening to knock her out.

Dana's heart thumped as she fell onto her backside. Slightly flushed out.

They were gone, like Marie had wanted. Those poor boys. They hadn't deserved...

Dana exhaled loudly, gradually picking herself off the floor. Marie had better not have hurt another one. She had better not. She hadn't had to listen to the cries and whimpers of George and Stephen. Their pleas. Dana approached the sink, scrubbing her hands as hard as she could. It didn't matter that she had worn gloves; her hands would never be rid of this filth.

Dana swallowed.

All those years ago – the others couldn't know about it. About Terry. She dried her hands then took out her phone.

It's done.

Since Marie had asked. Dana glanced between the toilet and her phone, her hand still shaking.

* * *

Nathan stood before the podium in the assembly hall. He cleared his throat as he looked at each student and teacher before him. Some already knew why they were here. Even though only some knew, everyone was silent. Some students merely glanced around at others.

'Morning, everyone.'

Since it could hardly be called a good one.

'Morning, Mr Byrne,' the students and teachers replied in unison.

'I'd like to take some time this morning to talk about our two Year Nine students, George Doyle and Stephen Mulgrew, who both suddenly died on Tuesday and yesterday. Some of you will have been good friends with both or either boy, and I understand that this loss will be difficult for you. It will be difficult for all of us. Please remember that you aren't alone, and that there is always someone here in Sandford College to talk to. Whether at the beginning or end of the school day; at break or lunch time. Even after this assembly. The school counsellor. Your form teacher,

Head of Year, the Head of Pastoral Care, Mrs Gordon-'

Some students looked to Marie as she nodded.

'-or even any of the classroom assistants. We are here for you. Following this assembly, your individual form teachers will provide additional sources of support that you may wish to make use of. I thank you all for your time this morning and this profoundly sad time.'

Nathan made his way off the stage. He had meant every word, as, without a doubt, did the rest of the teaching staff.

* * *

Beep, beep.

Dana removed her phone from her pocket.

I need you to do something.

Not another one. It had only been a week. Jesus Christ, not another-

What is it?

Dana looked at the screen, ridden with anxiety as she waited for the reply.

The CCTV footage. Get rid of it.

She didn't know how to, at least not-

Marie, I don't think it gets checked very often.

No one had. Did Marie think diff-

Get rid of it. I don't care how.

Obviously.

No one's going to be looking at it.

And no one had. Not since last Easter.

Get fucking rid of it.

Dana typed out her reply. Deleted it, then rewrote it.

Okay.

Dana sighed, then set her phone aside and put her hands over her face.

SIX

Marie climbed onto the double bed beside Eric, who was already sitting up watching the television on the dresser. The tail-end of an older *Midsomer Murders* episode. Really he was just waiting for *Law & Order: UK* to come on. Marie tucked her hair behind her ear, then straightened up her pillow.

'Hadn't you seen this one before?'

Eric nodded.

'Aye, about three times. Fourth's the charm, eh?'

Marie lifted her phone from the bedside table. Set to silent, of course.

'But you really prefer the UK version of that other show?' she asked, looking at her phone as it buzzed.

What time tomorrow?

'Anything with Bradley Walsh is always worth it.'

'Oh yeah?'

Just the usual. See you then, darling.

Eric nodded.

'That was sad about those two boys from your school.'

Marie looked at him.

'Aw, yeah,' she said with the same sombre tone as her husband. 'Always is when you lose them that way. You want the best for them, you know?'

Eric moved a little closer, putting his arm around her. She longed to slither free, but let his arm wrap around.

'Were they popular, yeah?'

'Aye. Quite. I suspect the funerals'll have quite a turnout.'

Eric nodded.

'You'll be back late tomorrow, won't you, love? Or is it Thursday?'

'Yep, tomorrow. Probably about the same time. Another meeting with a parent.'

Eric chuckled, just as Marie rested her head on his shoulder. He kissed her on the cheek.

'"Same old, same old", says you.'

'Yep.'

The much-awaited opening scene for *Law & Order: UK* appeared on screen.

Eric smiled.

'Ooh. looks like a good one.'

* * *

Dana leaned towards the computer monitor. Moving the mouse around the screen subconsciously. She was about to reboot it for a second time, just like Amanda McGreevy's laptop tomorrow. The problem would be something painstakingly obvious - it always was.

Marie had already gone home, of course. Just like yesterday. And the day before. Tomorrow would probably be even earlier.

Knock, knock.

Dana turned. Cathryn stood in the doorway.

'I got your note,' she said brightly. 'What's up, is it just about my laptop, yeah?'

Dana paused, then sighed.

'It's not, no. That, uh, that text I sent you back on Tuesday, it was meant for Marie. I was just a bit frantic after the whole thing, I-'

'I'm sorry, Dana, I thought it was just about work or something. I didn't-'

'You don't know anything about it?'

'About what?'

Pause.

'Those, uh, those kids. I didn't want to do it.'

'Do what? Do you mean those two students who died?'

Dana took a sharp intake of breath, glancing at the growing confusion in Cathryn's face.

'She told me to.'

'Told you to what?'

'She didn't want them to snitch, she made me do it.'

Cathryn stared at Dana.

'Dana, what are you... Are you telling me you...you did something to them?'

'She didn't want them to tell.'

Cathryn froze.

'She pushed him,' Dana continued, the words tumbling out. 'but it was an accident, she said.'

'And you didn't report it?'

'She didn't mean to do it. She got angry and-'

'Dana, why didn't you report it in the first place?'

'I-I couldn't let her tell them...tell them about my... She said it was an accident but then she went and did it again to another, and then got me to...'

Cathryn took a step back. Dana shot her several glances.

'Does Marie know about this,' Cathryn asked, 'does she know you sent that text to me?'

Dana shook her head. 'No.'

Cathryn put her hand to her mouth, exhaling deeply. Dana couldn't bear the painful silence.

'Jesus. Oh, Jesus Christ, Dana, what the hell have you done?'

Dana bowed her head.

'When she came in the second time, I knew, I *knew* it wasn't an accident. She was too calm, she was...'

Pause.

'What was it that Marie threatened to tell other people about?'

Dana shook her head, visibly trembling.

'Oh, come on, Dana.'

Dana looked to the floor. Cathryn put her hand against her hip.

'You've got me in all of this now as well, for god's sake,' she sniped. 'What is it you don't want people to know?'

Dana combed her hand back through her hair several times, still trembling. Some moments passed. Cathryn sighed.

'And it's just the two she's done this to?'

Dana nodded.

'And she definitely doesn't know you sent-'

'No.'

Cathryn nodded briefly, sighing again.

'Jesus. Oh, Jesus Christ.'

She stepped back.

'We will have to tell Nathan at some point. We will. Not yet, but-'

Dana nodded. Cathryn put her hand on Dana's arm.

'Tell me - text me - when she does it again. Yeah?'

Dana nodded again. Because there wasn't an ounce of doubt that Marie would.

* * *

'Oh, honestly, Alison. I thought we were going to have to do it all by hand.'

Marie laughed, as did Alison Grant, as the two women stood just outside the assembly hall.

'That's crazy,' Alison replied. 'Looks like we might have our work cut out for the rest of the week.'

Both women rolled their eyes.

'The joys, eh?'

Alison chuckled a little before clearing her throat.

'Kyle Parkin came to me yesterday,' she said quietly, 'fairly upset about your lad George Doyle. Had to keep him at the back of my class for the afternoon.'

Marie shook her head, sighing.

'They were good friends, too. It's awful, isn't it?'

Alison nodded.

'See you period seven, Marie.'

'See you.'

Alison walked towards the foyer, while Marie headed for the corridor leading to the main staircase.

'Miss?'

She turned. A boy as tall as her stood next to the wall.

'Yes, Shane?'

'Would I be able to get a new homework diary?'

'What's happened to your current one?'

'A couple of other boys wrecked it. Threw it down down the toilet.'

Marie nodded.

'Right,' she said softly. 'I'll try and get that sorted as soon as I can. Do you know what boys did it?'

Shane nodded.

'Okay, come to me at lunch and give me their names, and I'll speak with them. All right?'

Another nod.

'Just come at the beginning.'

'Okay, Miss.'

Shane walked off down the Languages corridor. Marie continued up the corridor and to the main staircase. She climbed the steps, turning left to another corridor, walking down until she reached a door at the end. Marie removed a set of keys from her blazer pocket, unlocked it, then entered. She approached a monitor which was split into four images. Paul the building supervisor seemed more than happy to show her how to work it. Probably didn't care why she had asked to in the first place. Three days on. Dana had better done it.

Marie looked at the top left image. Clicked a few buttons on the keyboard below. Looked again to see her room. On *that* day. Clicked for several minutes. George Doyle didn't appear. At all. Marie clicked again.

One week later. No sign of Stephen Mulgrew. At all. Good.

Marie smiled, then reverted the image back to today's date and left.

Good.

* * *

Dana rolled onto her left side. Then her right. Then her left. She pulled the bed cover over her. Closed her eyes.

Off and on for who knew how long? Siobhan wouldn't be here for another four days. Why couldn't it be sooner? No. It was just as well, actually.

'Why don't you go back and leave me alone?!'

Dana lay flat on her back. Breathed in and out as she stared at the ceiling.

'Go back to him!'

Terry.

Dana rubbed her eyes, feeling them well up. She hadn't meant it. Not a word.

Why didn't she just tell Cathryn there and then, instead of...

Why didn't she just-

Dana raised her arm and dragged her knuckles down the wall. Then up. Then down. Over and over.

SEVEN

Cathryn stood in the doorway of Jake's room. He sat on his bed.

'I don't expect you to tell me everything.'

Jake didn't answer.

'So you and Jessica, then. I'm glad you were going to tell me.'

Jake turned, eyes widening slightly.

'Your dad told me.'

Jake looked at her.

'It's nothing to do with that,' he sniped.

'No?'

'No.'

Cathryn crossed her arms, leaning against the doorframe.

'And you're going to say it's not because of this either?' she said, motioning to her head.

'It's not.'

'You don't talk to me, you go out of your way not to see me, for the last however many months, and somehow still expect me not to notice? Oh come on, Jake.'

He shot up.

'Don't start on at me like I'm one of your students,' he spat. 'If she wants to start a-'

'You've only been together about seven months-'

'Nine.'

'-nine months. And now you suddenly want to actually wise-up and-'

'What's wrong with that?!'

Cathryn paused, though not shaken by Jake's harsh tone.

'Nothing,' she said, a little more flatly than intended. 'Nothing. It's just quite a bit out of the blue, Jake.'

'You want me to stay in this place for the rest of my life?'

'Oh, wise up. Of course not.'

'Why don't you just get off my back like Dad does, then? You've obviously got an issue with-'

'I don't, Jake. I mean, if you feel you're ready for all this-'

'I am,' Jake shot back. 'I bloody am.'

Cathryn raised an eyebrow.

'Yeah? Yeah?'

'Yes!'

Cathryn stood up straight.

'When did you decide?'

'What?'

'That you were going to be a parent? Was it long before your dad told me?'

'No.'

'Really?'

'Yeah.'

'Right. Well, if you think you're ready...'

Cathryn stepped back and closed the door. Gently as ever.

* * *

'I'm certain I did do it, Irene. Yesterday afternoon.'

Dana leaned over Irene Havers' desk, as they both looked at a set of speakers. It was likely the last thing Havers wanted to be dealing with, with exam time beginning next month. Havers kept her arms folded, but meant well.

'Are you sure? I still haven't been getting anything out of them since Monday.'

Dana fiddled about with several leads. Of course she had, it was-

'Yes, I've... Right, play your...'

Havers pressed a button. Nothing.

Dana heaved out a sigh, combing her hand back through her hair.

'Sorry about that, Irene. Bit of a late night last night.'

Havers smiled, laughing quietly.

'Ah, it's fine, Dana,' she said brightly. 'Happens to the best of us. Been trying to catch up on my kip, myself.'

Dana nodded. Thankfully, Havers often took things as they came.

She glanced at Dana's hand.

'That looks a bit sore.'

Dana looked at her index and middle fingers on her left hand, which were wrapped in bandage.

'Ah, yeah. Just a bit of an accident with the stove, that's all.'

Havers nodded.

'Right,' Dana continued as if the previous exchange had never happened. 'Well, I'll get these sorted as soon as.'

'Thanking you.'

Dana unplugged the leads, lifting them along with the speakers, then left.

And Marie was none the bloody wiser. Somehow she was going home each night and sleeping soundly with Eric. And would probably do the same even if she was in a cell. *If* she was. She'd refuse to go down - put those families through *months* of unimaginable hell. Dana needed to hold on. She had to. For their sakes. For Cathryn's sake.

For everyone's sake.

* * *

Dana lay on the sofa. She placed her hand over her eyes.

The doorbell rang.

Dana peeled herself from the sofa and walked out to the front door. Opened it.

'Marie?'

Marie stepped inside; Dana stepped back as the door shut. Marie grabbed Dana's shoulders and threw her against the floor. Dana squirmed as Marie straddled her then pulled down her trousers. Then her pants.

'Marie...'

Dana grimaced, moaning quietly as something pushed into her vagina. Squeezed her eyes shut, scrunching up her face, feeling Marie's...Marie's fingers moving around inside. Over and over.

'Marie, please...Mar...'

'You like it. I know you do.'

Dana couldn't look...caught Marie's grin, as the fingers pushed deeper. She brought up her hand, which was almost immediately pinned to the floor.

Her fear gripped even the slightest attempt to speak in a vice.

Marie's fingers...pulled out.

Dana looked to the floor, shaking badly as Marie let go and climbed to her feet. She felt her eyes begin to well, keeping her gaze on the floor as she heard Marie walk to the door, then leave.

Dana jolted awake. Rubbed her eyes, breathing rapidly. Thank fucking hell this was a single bed. Sleep had been eluding her for however long lately. And then when Dana finally could, even just for a bit. She put her trembling hand over her vaginal area. Removed her trousers, opened the top drawer in her dresser and grabbed a fresh pair of pants. Dana held the old pair between her finger and thumb and headed into the bathroom, dumping them into the bin. She approached the sink and scrubbed her hands. Over and over.

* * *

Marie strolled into her kitchen. Sighed, almost quite contentedly. Once again, Eric wouldn't be home until later. Just as before. All the better, of course. If only it could have been Harvey, then she could do him like it was the first time all over again. Eric would never know. Harvey had recently gotten a new neighbour, but it didn't matter. It hadn't spoiled this evening, so it definitely wasn't gong to spoil things in the long run.

Where had this handsome toy boy been hiding this last century? At least, that was how long Marie's marriage had felt like.

Marie had never felt so...oh, she still didn't have the word. She slipped off her jacket then headed upstairs.

EIGHT

'Dana.'

She turned from her desk, moving the projector she was working on to the side. Cathryn stood in the office doorway. Dana had made it this far through the work day – the work week – without a peep from Marie. She could have been watching both Dana and Cathryn on the cameras. Especially now.

'Where should we start, then?'

Dana paused, as Cathryn approached her, seeming just a little slimmer.

'Cameras?'

Cathryn nodded, but sighed.

'She'll have had the footage wiped, I imagine.'

Dana opened the first drawer on the left of her desk, taking out a flash drive.

'So she thinks.'

Cathryn's face lit up.

'Oh, brilliant. Is there much?'.

'Hopefully enough.'

'Oh, Dana, this has to be,' Cathryn said quite confidently. 'I think we've got that...'

'Where should I leave it?'

Cathryn paused.

Held onto the cord wrapped around her neck as it dug in against her flesh.

'Top drawer in my desk, along with anything else you have.'

Dana briefly squeezed her eyes shut. Cathryn stood opposite her, just as before. Dana nodded.

'She did ask me to. Because, you know, why...why wouldn't I?'

Cathryn nodded.

Lay face-down on top of Marie on the floor, both of them naked, as Marie fingered her.

Dana's eyes shut then opened. A fully-clothed Cathryn watched her.

'Don't you be staying too late. All right?'

Dana nodded. 'Yeah.'

Cathryn patted her on the shoulder.

'One step at a time, eh?'

*　*　*

I don't want to go on, Cathryn. I suspect by the time you read this, I'll be gone. I can't deal with any of it. I don't

Dana set down the pen. She couldn't write any more. Couldn't tell Siobhan about any of it. Where would she even start? Where would Cathryn start, if she told her?

'Please, Dana. Please!'

Dana looked up.

George and Stephen hung from the lights before her. Their pale helpless faces stared.

Dana squeezed her eyes shut, then looked. The boys were gone. She looked at the page. Picked up her pen.

I don't know if you'll catch her. She's already

The pen clattered against the table.

Oh, Terry.

*　*　*

'How much has she been worrying about me?'

Adrian and Jake walked along the park pathway. Not terribly busy for this hour. Jake blew a ring of smoke from his cigarette.

'Too much would be an understatement. But you know, there's work and that, too.'

'I want to tell her, Dad, but she just wouldn't approve.'

Adrian sighed.

'Don't you think it's a bit soon to be wanting kids?' He asked. 'Would you not want to wait until it's at least been a year?'

Jake puffed again.

'You know why I want to, Dad.'

They continued along the path, as other people passed occasionally.

'She's been up to her eyes with work lately, and you,' Adrian said. 'But I don't know, there might be something else.'

'Like what?'

'I don't know, but even with all of that, I don't think she's been... Oh, I don't know, Jake. It's something.'

'I didn't-'

If Adrian had smoked, he would have snatched Jake's cigarette off him and puffed his brains out.

'It's gotten worse. The cancer. I think seven months was being generous. I know you don't want her to die, son, I know you don't want to see that. There's only so long I can be your go-between.'

'I know.'

'She thinks you're making it all about you. I know you know that.'

'I do want to tell her, Dad. I want her to know that I want to be settled and get with my life before she dies, and that she can stop worrying about me.'

'She never would.'

'I know.'

Jake took a long drag on his cigarette. The two men stopped at a bench and sat down. Watched their surroundings for while.

'What's Jessica said about it?' Adrian asked.

Jake sighed.

'She wishes I'd tell Mum, as well. She's not frustrated, though. She feels bad for all of us.'

Adrian nodded. He and Jake both knew they'd have to go back home at some point.

'Don't leave it too long, okay?'

NINE

'It's an easy enough rhyme to remember. Divorced; beheaded; died. Divorced; beheaded; survived. Good way to remember what happened, as well.'

Marie set aside a folder as 8H continued to copy down from the slide on the whiteboard. Her second favourite class. Many of them seemed to have her pegged as their favourite teacher - at least that's what she had overheard.

'Did he really call one of them an ugly mare, Miss?'

Marie nodded.

'Yes. Yes, he did. And went straight back home afterwards.'

Marie chuckled into herself at the murmurs among the students.

Knock, knock.

'Come in.'

Half the class turned their heads as Dana walked in, holding a small box.

'That's it ready for period five and six,' she said, handing the box to Marie. 'You know where I am if there's any problems.'

Marie nodded. 'Thanks, Dana.'

Dana said nothing, then left again. Marie set the box aside. The class quietened down again.

'Right, folks,' she said brightly. 'On to Catherine of Aragon.'

* * *

Cathryn closed her storeroom door and sat down inside. She placed a large brown envelope on one of the shelves before her, opened it, removed the flash drive and plugged it into her laptop. Pressed 'play'. Saw Marie and George Doyle. Marie pushing him. It seemed like it was done without thinking. Frankly, it was difficult to tell, no matter how many times Cathryn replayed it. Then Marie and Stephen Mulgrew. Marie shoving him against the wall. Hard. If the first time was genuinely an overreaction, why had she done it again? Was it... Had something happened in the past between her and Dana? It was the only logical reason she could think of. Except nothing was logical, let alone justifiable, about any of this. Perhaps Cathryn could ask

Dana the next time they saw each other. She would have to tell Cathryn at some point.

Cathryn reached into the envelope and produced a small device and earphones. A note was attached.

This should be what gets her. She had and has no idea.

Cathryn stuck the earphones in and pressed 'play'.

She knew she wasn't going to like whatever she heard. She just knew.

* * *

'What time's the class on until, Miss?'

As Cathryn approached the staffroom, she stopped and turned to Rebecca Gallagher. One of her better students, both academically and sense-wise.

'Shouldn't be any later than half-four. All right?'

Rebecca nodded.

'Am I down for higher or foundation tier, again?'

'Higher as always, Rebecca.'

'Oh, okay. Thanks, Miss.'

'See you up there shortly.'

'Yep.'

Cathryn nodded as Rebecca headed up the corridor in the direction of her classroom. If even a quarter of

Cathryn's class showed up, it would be another little victory. That quarter would be the likes of Rebecca. The next while would be a little bit of a relief. Not before she had a cigarette, though.

Beep, beep.

Cathryn took out her phone.

I'm ready to talk. About Terry.

* * *

Marie walked through the living room door, humming quietly. She sat down on the sofa, hearing Eric getting ready in kitchen. The Slovakians had been gone for a good while, so no shouting at four o'clock in the morning. Eric had considered writing them a polite note, but he and Marie both knew there was no point.

'I'll be back at about seven, maybe eight, tomorrow. Depends on your man's mood.'

Eric approached Marie, in his full suit and tie attire.

'You give that Maguire one hell.'

Eric chuckled, planting a kiss on Marie's cheek.

'You've been rather...happy lately. You up for a promotion or something like that?'

'Oh, aye. Head of my department,' Marie joked. 'Nah. Theresa Bothwell from Geography's tying the knot. About three months from now.'

She wasn't.

'Really? We invited, then?'

Since it had already been fifteen years ago, no.

'It's a given. Has he really been running you ragged, lately?'

Eric sucked the air, folding his arms. Not a pose that suited him.

'Nothing too taxing.'

Marie nodded. Eric grabbed his jacket and headed out to the front door. Marie reached into her pocket-

'See you, love!'

'Yeah.'

-removed her phone, just as the door slammed shut. Typed.

I'll be over in about an hour, darling. We'll make a night of it.

* * *

Cathryn and Dana entered Dana's living room, then sat down on opposite ends of the sofa. Dana looked between Cathryn and the floor numerous times.

'Just take your time, Dana, okay?'

Her gaze stayed on the floor. She combed back her hair.

'I was sixteen, and he was about fifteen,' Dana began gradually. 'Terry was living with his dad. His mum was out of the picture. He and I would hang out sometimes. But... Every now and then, he'd tell me about his dad, moan about something he had done to him.'

'Like abuse?'

Dana nodded.

'I couldn't understand why he was telling me. 'I said... I said "just tell him to stop". I didn't know what his dad was...was doing to him, and I kept telling Terry the same thing.'

Dana paused, rubbing her eyes.

'We got... We got...into an argument,' she continued. 'Really screamed at each other. I really didn't know what my uncle had been doing to him because he was always so nice to me - you know, inviting me for lunch, and that - so why would he have been hitting Terry, keeping his fingers against the stove?'

Cathryn had kept her eyes on Dana, glancing at Dana's fingers, while the latter seemingly couldn't bear to look up.

'I really got sick of it,' Dana continued. 'We were outside my house. I was fed up with it, I said "why don't you just... Why don't you just do back to your dad and leave me the hell alone?".

71

Dana raised her hand to her face, wiping her eyes, and exhaled loudly.

'He had nowhere else to go, so he did. Two days later, I found out my uncle had...had...'

Dana sniffed, rubbing her red-rimmed eyes.

'He'd raped him. Then Terry killed himself. In the same way I had to make George and Stephen's deaths look. Marie and Siobhan both said it wasn't my fault.'

'It's not.'

Dana looked at Cathryn.

'It was your uncle's problem if he couldn't keep his hands off Terry. Not yours. Okay, you spoke out of turn, but you didn't mean it, did you? It was a mistake.'

Dana paused. Still she looked ashamed.

'Marie, she promised not to tell anyone else. It was only a few years after we had met.'

'When did you meet?'

'When we were both seventeen. And I don't think she had, because no one else ever said anything about it. She let me stay in hers for a couple of nights. "I *know* it wasn't your fault, but...".'

Cathryn paused, watching as the other woman wiped her nose. What an absolute...

'When'd you tell Siobhan?'

Dana exhaled.

'Not long after we had met. I-I just wanted to get it out of the way.'

'Was... I'm guessing she was all right with it – given she's still with you.'

'It took her a while...to process it,' Dana said softly. 'She came back to the house later on, so... I think she must have been.'

Cathryn nodded.

'Okay. Okay. You've done really well in telling me all this, Dana. You don't have to tell Nathan, and I won't tell him. All right?'

Dana looked at the floor. Nodded.

'Do you want to get Siobhan over, just even for tonight?'

'She'll be over tomorrow.'

'Okay.'

Cathryn stood up.

'Thanks again, Dana, for telling me.'

TEN

'Sharon, will Nathan just be in his office this afternoon, you know, after the school day?'

Between enduring 10R, her laptop going on the blink, and having to break up an altercation between three students, Cathryn's morning had been a *long* one and lunchtime could not have come quick enough. Not before she did this, though.

Sharon turned to her computer screen.

'I think he's got a meeting with a parent until about four. But I can tell him you were looking him, if you want?'

Cathryn nodded, as Sharon produced a post-it note and pen.

'Aye, just want to see him in his office.'

Sharon finished writing, giving Cathryn a thumbs-up. She walked away, clearing her throat. Her stomach sank, though probably not as much as Dana's would tomorrow. Where did Cathryn start? And how was she going to tell Adrian?

* * *

Marie entered the staffroom holding several files under her arm. She set them down just as Cathryn entered from the back room, typically holding a mug of coffee.

'I think Alison wants to move the meeting next week forward, Cathryn.'

Cathryn moved to the sink, emptying the mug's remaining contents.

'What day?'

'Monday. Half four.'

'Right, okay.'

'Fairly short notice, I know.'

Cathryn nodded, then placed the mug on the drainer. Marie lifted the files and turned to her locker, skimmed them before putting them inside.

* * *

Dana stood in the doorway of Cathryn's room.

'I'm, uh, I'm going now.'

Cathryn turned from her desk, holding several files. She set them down.

'Still just on your own, yeah?'

'Uh-huh.'

'I'll tell him later before I go myself, okay?'

Dana nodded. Cathryn approached her.

'I've got the flash drive and recording hidden away,' she continued. 'Just leave the other stuff you've got in my locker like we agreed, all right?'

Cathryn watched as Dana sighed.

'Try and sleep, if you can.'

'There's no fucking point.'

Cathryn placed her hand on Dana's shoulder.

'I know, I know. But we've got her. We've got her, Dana.'

Dana exhaled. Cathryn let go and turned back to her desk.

* * *

Dana entered the staffroom. Marie stood by her locker with her coat on, spotting the other woman in the corner of her eye, but didn't look at her.

'No meetings, then? Phone calls, or that sort of thing?'

Marie retrieved her bag and shut the locker door.

'No.'

Said curtly.

'Not like you. Though neither is-'

'How are you getting home?'

'Don't change the subject.'

Marie placed the strap of her bag over her shoulder.

'Are you getting a taxi?'

'Marie, don't chan-'

'Looks like it's going to rain. I'll drop you off – won't say a word about Terry – if you do the same for me.'

Dana's stare hardened at even the mention of the name. For fuck's sake, Marie.

'Fine.'

Marie nodded, heading towards the door.

'Meet you in a bit.'

* * *

Cathryn buttoned up her jacket. Five minutes past five. She stood before her open locker, rubbing the back of her head. Longing for a cigarette.

'Home time at last, then, Cath?'

Cathryn turned. Alison Grant walked from the back room over to a nearby chair.

'Oh, yeah. Long day, you know? Can finally have something to eat when I do.'

Alison smiled, then sighed briefly.

'Got to cover Mandy's last three classes tomorrow,' she heaved out. 'God help us.'

The two women exchanged a chuckle, and Cathryn closed her locker and put her bag over her shoulder.

'See you in the morning, Alison.'

'See you.'

Cathryn exited the staffroom, then headed out through the main doors and towards her car. She climbed in, dumped her bag beside her and took out her phone. Began typing.

Dana, I spoke to Nathan, told him everything I could. He will want to see you in the morning, just as I'd said. Try to get some sleep, and just remember, we've got her.

Cathryn pressed 'send', replaced her phone. Now to tell Adrian when she finally came home. Like with Nathan, it had to happen at some point.

Cathryn started her car.

Nothing more for Dana could be done. For now.

ELEVEN

Cathryn entered through the main doors, glancing at the principal's office.

'Morning, Cathryn.'

She nodded to Sharon, then headed over into the staffroom. Around a third of her colleagues were also present. Including Marie.

Graham Niblock passed by.

'Morning, Cath.'

'Morning.'

She approached her locker, placed her bag inside, then took out her phone. Still no reply. It had been quite the conversation with Adrian last night. He hadn't seemed *too* mad. Maybe he thought there was no point, with the cancer and that. Jake, however...

How would either Cathryn or Adrian tell him? Maybe he would understand best if the police told him. If it came from someone other than his own mother, anyway. Cathryn removed her jacket and hung it over the nearest chair.

'Want a cuppa, Cath?'

She turned to the sound of Amanda McGreevy's voice, who gripped a freshly brewed tea.

'Aye, yeah, sure. Just leave it next to my seat, I'll be back in a minute. Ta.'

Amanda flashed a smile. Cathryn exited the staffroom and headed over into the toilet, passing numerous students. She looked back to her phone, at her last message to Dana. There was still twenty minutes to go. At this point, how likely was it that Dana was still just running late? Cathryn sighed quietly. She wasn't sure exactly when, but she had definitely seen it coming. Nathan was going to love this. Cathryn replaced her phone and headed back to the staffroom. She would need this coffee.

* * *

Marie felt her fingers tense up as she typed on her computer. She glanced at the empty chairs in her room. Fortunately not for much longer. Marie breathed in and out several times, doing her best to stay composed. Easily done. She scoffed quietly, flexing her fingers. Again. And again.

Then continued typing.

* * *

The clock struck ten minutes past nine. Cathryn walked along the corridor, gradually approaching Nathan's office. Exhaled. Knocked.

'Come in.'

She opened the door.

'Ah, Cathryn.'

Nathan was standing at the shelves behind his desk, looking rather expectant.

'Dana still hasn't turned up,' Cathryn began. 'I'm not sure if she's still just running late and maybe hasn't been able to phone the school, for whatever reason. I mean, her phone's not switched off.'

Nathan sat down. Cathryn caught his look.

'We could maybe try phoning one of her family. Her partner Siobhan, she might know.'

'She'd be Dana's next of kin, wouldn't she?'

Cathryn nodded.

'They're not living together, but we can still try and phone her.'

'Okay. Will you get onto Sharon and...'

Cathryn nodded, taking out a small device and earphones from her pocket.

'This is the other bit,' she said, handing it to him. 'Just listen to it while I'm away here. You'll need a bit of time.'

Nathan clutched the device and earphones. 'Right.'

Cathryn turned and left. She walked towards reception. Sharon sat behind her computer, typing.

'Sharon, do you know if we've got a number for Dana's partner, at all?'

The other woman clicked her mouse several times, then typed again.

'Let's see... Yep, here we are. Siobhan Foreman.'

'Is that up-to-date?'

'I believe so.'

'Great. Do you mind if I-'

'No, go ahead.'

Cathryn lifted the receiver and dialled.

'Hello, is that Siobhan?'

'Aye. Is that Cathryn?'

'It is, yeah.'

'Aw, hiya, Cathryn. What's up?'

'Do you know if Dana's at home or not, Siobhan? It's just the she hasn't turned up for work.'

'No idea. Haven't heard from her since the other morning.'

'Would you be able to go over and check, at all?'

'I'm just at the shop, about fifteen minutes away, but I can do that and get back to you if that's-'

'Sure, that's not a problem. Thanks, Siobhan.'

'All right. Bye.'

'Bye.'

Cathryn replaced the receiver.

'Sharon, could you keep a line open for about the next twenty minutes? She's going to call me back.'

Sharon nodded. 'No problem.'

'Ta.'

Cathryn walked back towards Nathan's office. Stopped, just for a little longer. It had to be done – Cathryn wished it hadn't but unfortunately Nathan needed to know the whole, ugly, truth. She knocked.

'Come in.'

Cathryn entered, closing the door gently.

Nathan sat up behind his desk, appearing to fidget with his fingers. He didn't look up.

'I got speaking to Siobhan, I...'

Still he didn't look up.

'I can't... I can't believe this.'

Cathryn nodded.

'I'm sorry, Nathan.'

Nathan had seemingly noticed her nervous expression.

'How'd that...'

'Got speaking to Siobhan, who's away to check now,' Cathryn replied. 'Shouldn't be too long.'

Nathan nodded, putting his hands together on his desk.

'You, uh, you look a bit...'

Cathryn rubbed her mouth.

'I don't mean to worry you any more, Nathan, but, uh, but... I think Dana might possibly...possibly be dead.'

Nathan sat up as straight as his chair would allow, as if to ask 'what?'

'I think... I mean, I don't know... I noticed a number of days ago that she'd burnt her fingers – in fact, Irene Havers did as well when Dana was looking at her speakers. She'd obviously tried to pass it off as an accident, but with all of this going on...'

'Right.'

I texted her last night – even phoned her again this morning, and no reply. All that stuff, including this, which I showed you yesterday. She really wanted to bring down Marie. As do I.'

Nathan drummed his fingers.

'And the rest of the stuff, it's somewhere safe?'

'Yes.'

Nathan sat back. Exhaled loudly.

'Okay. *Okay.* I'm going to get cover arranged for your classes. Let me know when-'

'Sure.'

Cathryn turned and left. Unfortunately, the likelihood that her worst fears would be confirmed hung over every other thought – even those about Jake. Cathryn entered the staffroom and headed for her bag. She dug around and lifted out a water bottle. Took a few sips. For some reason, part of her felt as though Marie would walk through the door. Highly unlikely, of course. She was carrying on with her day like usual. Keeping everyone else oblivious to the monster that she was. Cathryn took a few more sips. Two families were ruined, and now along with two more, would be all over again. Ten minutes passed.

'Cathryn?'

She looked as Sharon appeared. Cathryn nodded and followed her to reception, inhaling.

Cathryn pushed open Nathan's door. It seemed that he hadn't moved since the last time, which had felt like forever.

'Siobhan's just spoke with me. She found Dana and...'

Cathryn exhaled.

'I think we should tell them now, Nathan,' she continued. 'Dana *is* dead, but I...I don't think it was by her own hand.'

'What?'

'Siobhan said there was...was blood in the kitchen, and she found Dana lying in her bedroom with...uh, with her head bashed in.'

Nathan sat back, looking at his desk for several moments, evidently trying to comprehend everything. Just as Cathryn was.

'How's Siobhan?'

'Did my best to keep her calm, but obviously...'

'Yeah. She'll just be waiting for the police, yes?'

Cathryn nodded. Nathan rubbed his hands together.

'Okay. Get on to them now.'

TWELVE

Marie closed her laptop. She lifted several workbooks and headed to her storeroom. One more hour to go, then she could leave. Maybe even just thirty minutes. Marie couldn't have gotten out of that house quick enough. Nobody would find Dana, just yet. Not in her bedroom. Marie had cleaned up the blood enough. Hadn't she? They could only take her word about it all, just as it should have been.

Knock, knock.

'Oh, hi, Sharon.'

The other woman flashed a smile.

'Alison has got those worksheets for you up in B8.'

'Ah, great.'

Marie followed Sharon out of the room, and they turned right up the corridor.

'See you soon, Marie.'

'All right, see you.'

Sharon turned left towards a set of double doors, while Marie continued along the corridor. They wouldn't find Dana yet. They couldn't. Marie gradually reached the last door on the left side, opened it and walked through.

Stopped.

Two police officers stood before Marie. Cathryn and Nathan stood in the corner.

'Marie Gordon,' one officer began as the other walked behind her, placing cuffs around her wrists. 'I'm arresting you on suspicion of the conspiracy to murder George Doyle and Stephen Mulgrew, and on suspicion of the murder of Dana Chesterson. You do not have to say anything. But, it may harm your defence if you do not mention when questioned something which you later rely on in court. Anything you do say may be given in evidence.'

Marie looked at Cathryn and Nathan – Cathryn, particularly – as the officers lead her away. The door opened. An officer appeared.

'Just whenever you're ready to, you'll have to come down to the station for a statement, okay?'

Cathryn and Nathan nodded. The officer left.

Cathryn sighed, rubbing her eyes.

They exchanged a look. Dana was right, Marie would deny it all – why else would she have been so calm when being taken away? Nathan headed towards the door and Cathryn followed. They walked along the corridor and down the stairs. Saying nothing. Neither could as they continued along another corridor, eventually reaching the staffroom. Nathan held open the door, letting Cathryn through. She headed towards the sink, lifting one of several glasses beside it.

'Bloody hell.'

Still Nathan was silent. Cathryn watched as water filled the glass, then took a few sips. She set down the glass, then-

Felt her chest tighten slightly. As she brought her hand up, she heaved out several breaths.

'Cathryn, are you all right?'

She raised her hand to her neck. Nathan grabbed a nearby chair.

'Just you sit down.'

He helped lower her onto it. The room appeared slightly out of focus. She paused. Exhaled. The pain...began to fade away. Cathryn exhaled – with a little more ease, this time.

'Think... Think it's gone.'

Cathryn shook her head briefly, rubbing her eyes. She caught Nathan's look.

'You sure?'

'Think so.'

Cathryn began to push herself up from the chair, taking Nathan's hand. Gradually, she headed towards her locker and removed a small bag.

'Do you want to get Adrian to come for you?'

Cathryn placed it on a nearby chair.

'Yeah, sure. I'll phone him now.'

Nathan turned, ma-

Cathryn fell.

Nathan rushed towards her and took out his phone.

'Ambulance. I'm not sure, she's just collapsed. We're at Sandford College.'

He kept his eyes on the pale woman. Her eyes were closed; she lay still.

'I think... Oh god, I'm not sure...'

THIRTEEN

'What are you saying, Dana?'

She glared at Marie as the car continued along the road, growing closer to Dana's house. She caught Marie's sick little smile.

'You were just waiting, weren't you? The day I spilled it all, from then on you were just waiting. You knew I wouldn't...'

Dana heaved out a sigh. The car pulled up outside Dana's house. She removed her seatbelt, then pulled up the door lock.

'If you're going to start giving me lifts again, maybe think about washing that guy's cum off your seats first.'

Marie stared. Dana climbed out, heading up the pathway to her front door. Marie followed.

'You bitch, how do you know?'

Dana stopped briefly, glancing at Marie. Scoffed, as she removed her keys from her pocket, then continued on and unlocked the front door.

'How do you know?'

Dana stepped inside, ignoring Marie's cutting tone.

'I'm probably not the only one.'

Marie followed suit, closing the door as Dana continued down the hallway.

'And Siobhan and I aren't going to be the only ones who'll know about Terry.'

Dana exhaled loudly as she entered the kitchen; Marie right behind her.

'You never thought of their families, did you?' Dana sniped, lashing around to Marie. 'For twenty years, it's never fucking been about anyone other than *you*. And now that it's all completely in the shit, they're going to see you for who you really fucking are.'

Marie stepped back, clenching her fists.

'And you, Dana. Like they'll believe you.'

'Cathryn will.'

Marie paused.

'What?'

Dana didn't speak. For mere seconds, the two women locked eyes.

Marie bound towards Dana, grabbed her by the neck and threw her to the floor. Marie pressed her arm deep into Dana's throat. Dana swung at Marie's head, knocking her back. As Dana rushed to get back on her feet, Marie kicked out. Dana stumbled but stayed upright. She felt along the drawers beside her, pulling one open. She rummaged through it and produced a rolling pin. Marie stepped towards her. With both arms, Dana swung. Marie ducked. Dana swung harder. Marie ducked again.

'Stop it!'

Again. Marie moved back. Dana stepped forward and hurled the rolling pin at her.

Marie staggered back as it hit her hard across the chest.

'She's got it all, everything you did, on the cameras, Marie,' Dana spat. 'Even you telling me how to do it. They know.'

Marie's eyes darted. She looked at Dana, half-smiling. Started walking towards her.

'But not about your cousin. What you put him through.'

'They were kids.'

'Terry didn't deserve what you did to him.'

'Neither did those boys.'

'It was an accident, Dana. Both times. I told you.'

'Fucking stop it, Marie. You've got no-'

Thwack!

Dana jarred, then staggered back. Marie followed, clenching the rolling pin with both hands.

Thwack!

Dana crumpled to the floor. Amidst her cries, she raised her hands to her face as Marie swung down again and again with all her might. Again, as blood gushed out of Dana's skull. Again, each strike now harder than the last. Again, as-

Dana jolted, but didn't react. Her face was still; her eyes vacant.

Blood streamed into a pool around her head. Marie breathed heavily, still gripping the bloodied rolling pin. Her gaze darted. She climbed to her feet, as the rolling pin clattered against the floor. Looked at the woman below. Around the kitchen. At Dana. Bent down and lifted Dana by her arms, then began to drag her along the floor.

Sandford College Police Report - Verbatim Transcription

Evidence Type: audio recording

Speaker 1: Marie Gordon

Speaker 2: Dana Chesterson

[a car door opens then shuts]

Gordon: You do it tonight. [George] Doyle, then the second kid, Stephen Mulgrew, two days later. Because otherwise it's going to seem rather suspicious.

Chesterson: How do you know it won't look suspicious anyway?

Gordon: It won't.

Chesterton: What about what you did to them? They're not going to think that was an accident.

Gordon: Who's they? Because you're not telling the police, Dana. Their deaths will look like suicide if you do them the way I tell you.

[pause]

Chesterson: You—You hadn't molested either of them as-'

[*a slap is heard*]

Gordon: How dare you. That's another thing entirely.

Chesterson: It'd still be-

Gordon: You really think I'd get it on, that I'd fuck, any of those kids? Fucking wise up. George Doyle's a lost cause, just like Mulgrew. No one would know what to do with either of them in the real world.

Chesterson: What did you say to George? To Stephen?

Gordon: It doesn't matter.

Chesterson: It obviously does or we wouldn't be sitting here now, because you can't accept that you messed up.

Gordon: You still can't accept what Terry did wasn't your fault. We wouldn't be sitting here if you could.

Chesterson: You're the one who came to me because you overreacted. You should have just left it.

Gordon: Things get around that place like wildfire, Dana. You said it yourself.

Chesterson: But this wouldn't have.

Gordon: What happens to them will. What really happens. What <u>you</u> did to Terry.

[pause]

Chesterson: What—What do you want me to do to them?

Gordon: What you made Terry do.

[pause]

Chesterson: And you'll tell the rest of them, you'll reassure them, that they can talk to you, while you walk around with your hands soaked in George and Stephen's blood.

Gordon: It'll be you with-

Chesterton: I'm not doing it.

Gordon: Siobhan knows about this as well, then?

[pause]

Gordon: You don't want to break her little heart, I'm sure.

[pause]

Gordon: Let me know when it's done.

[*a car door is heard being opened, then Chesterson climbing out and closing the car door*]

End of recording.

Following her arrest and extensive interrogation, Marie Gordon pleaded guilty to and was convicted of two counts of assaulting a minor, the conspiracy to murder George Doyle and Stephen Mulgrew, and the murder of Dana Chesterson. She is currently serving a life sentence with a minimum tariff of thirty years.

Following her collapse, Cathryn Redmond was pronounced dead at the scene by paramedics, having suffered a massive heart attack. She was fifty-three.

Over one hundred people attended Cathryn's funeral, including Siobhan Foreman and Marie's ex-husband Eric. Six attendees, including Siobhan and Eric, were present at Dana's.

Since the funerals, Adrian, Eric, and Siobhan, meet up on occasion. All three attend therapy.

Jake Redmond subsequently quit smoking, and now lives with his girlfriend Jessica. They are now expecting their first child.

AFTERWORD

The main plot of *All That Matters* was one I had wanted to explore for a number of years. There were many alternate versions of just about every part of it. Maybe Marie could have found out about Cathryn knowing much earlier on. Maybe Cathryn and Jake would have patched things up. Perhaps Marie could actually have been lying about the incidents with George and Stephen. Who knows?

I endeavoured to keep the story as real as possible and avoid cliches as far as I could. From the moment her 'little problem' was established, I knew things were never going to end well for Dana. I also knew it would be too easy to kill off Marie and give the reader a certain satisfaction. She was much too full of her own importance and need for control to end her life, of course. Cathryn's ending, however, still hits the hardest for me. Though it was well-meaning, she pushed - worked herself much harder than she ever realised - throughout the story, at the worst cost. The signs were there – her anxiety and frustration about her son, and later Dana and Marie; the frequent smoking; doing the extra support classes for her students when she probably should have been reducing her workload – but, as is often the case, all in hindsight.

As it progressed, *All That Matters* kept growing darker and darker, certainly more than I had ever intended when first developing it. Perhaps that's what happens when a writer's frame of mind goes to a not-so-great place. What manifests inside it.

Just how far can someone be willing to go to protect their reputation? Just how often do situations like Marie's blatant abuse of authority towards George Doyle and Stephen Mulgrew, in schools and other places alike, slip through the cracks? To date, I think Marie Gordon holds the record for the most despicable antagonist I've ever created. Yes, Dana may have killed two innocent boys, but for Marie to use such a sensitive and traumatic event to get her to do so...

Of course, even though Dana did try to redeem herself by deciding quite early on that Marie needed stopped for good, it is understandable if you have absolutely zero sympathy for her. It is unsettling, however, to remember sometimes how many Marie Gordon's exist in the real world.

Some say honesty is the best policy, especially in a marriage. But even then, there are limits.

And now for a stiff drink.

Until the next time, reader.

ABOUT THE AUTHOR

Kayleigh Hughes first discovered her passion for writing stories in her teens, mainly drama, thriller, with the odd bit of comedy. She is the author of Meanwhile... and Bridging The Gap. When not immersed in her characters and their worlds, she is absorbing yet another piece of film or television trivia, or jamming on the guitar or bass.

Printed in Great Britain
by Amazon

30001781R00061